DISNEY

INFITY

W9-AXD-098

Copyright © 2015 Disney Enterprises, Inc. Pixar elements
© Disney/Pixar. All rights reserved. Published in the United
States by Random House Children's Books, a division of
Penguin Random House LLC, 1745 Broadway, New York, NY
10019, and in Canada by Random House of Canada, a division
of Penguin Random House Ltd., Toronto. Random House and
the colophon are registered trademarks of Penguin Random
House LLC.

The term OMNIDROID is used by permission of Lucasfilm Ltd.

randomhousekids.com
For more information on Disney Infinity, please visit:
Disney.com/Infinity

ISBN 978-0-7364-3424-9 (trade)
ISBN 978-0-7364-8245-5 (lib. bdg.)

Printed in the United States of America

10 9 8 7 6 5 4 3 2 1

DISNEY INFINITY

ICE RACE!

By Amy Weingartner
Illustrated by Fabio Laguna and James Gallego

Random House New York

Chapter 1

In the world of the Toy Box, a girl named Merida looked up. A muscular man dressed in a bright red Super suit roared through the sky on a hoverboard.

Merida gasped.

"Wait for us!" she shouted. Merida and her horse, Angus, had been following a girl with a long white braid who zoomed ahead of them, racing on a track of ice. Snow and ice were flying out behind her.

"Watch out—coming through!" called a voice. A young and very speedy racer, also in a red superhero suit, whizzed by at super speed.

"Hey," Merida called to the racer, "that big fella. You look just like—"

"Me?" said the muscular man in the Super suit, landing next to her. "That's because I'm his dad, Mr. Incredible. That's Dash."

Merida and Mr. Incredible stopped to look around. They both noticed the amazing racetrack stretched out before them.

"This is some interesting world you have here," said Mr. Incredible.

"I'm Merida. I'm not from here, but I know what you mean," Merida replied.

Merida had just been on a big adventure with lots of new friends she'd met in this place—the Toy Box. She had been following the mysterious white-haired girl when Mr. Incredible and Dash showed up.

"Angus and I were at home when we saw a shooting star, and it brought us here," Merida explained. "I was hoping to follow it home again when I saw you folks and decided to race after you."

"Dash and I saw a shooting star in Metroville, where we live, and followed it here," Mr. Incredible told her. "We're used to adventure. Everyone in our family is . . . Super."

Mr. Incredible nodded proudly in the direction of Dash, still racing along the track.

Merida jumped back on her horse. "Angus and I are going to try to catch up to them. The wonderful thing about this world is you can usually find gadgets or fancy karts to help you do things. Just look around!"

Merida and Angus galloped away, while Mr. Incredible found a monster truck. He tossed his hoverboard in the back and climbed into the vehicle, then pressed on the gas pedal and took off. In no time at all, he caught sight of the other three.

Dash was gaining on the girl. Merida was not far behind them.

The terrain that the track rolled through changed continuously. One minute they were racing through a wooded area. That would lead to an open green field. The black asphalt of the track became steeper, twisting and turning as it wound its way into some hills. Pine trees appeared, and then the ground on either side of the track began to look white and snowy.

"This is fun," said Mr. Incredible.

"That's what makes it an adventure, don't you think?" replied Merida.

"Watch out!" said Mr. Incredible. The

track had risen high off the ground. They had come to a long drop, which Angus handled easily. Mr. Incredible revved his engine and followed them. The mighty machine jumped the divide.

The other side of the jump was rocky and snowy. They could see mountains and what looked like a castle.

"This place amazes me!" said Merida. "You never know what you'll see next."

"Or *who*," said a voice. The white-haired girl suddenly appeared *behind* them. She was on a hoverboard. "I'm Elsa," she said.

"You were ahead of us! How did you do that?" asked Merida.

"I know all kinds of tricks," said Elsa. "And in this part of the Toy Box world, there are lots of ways to find adventure!"

"I'm Merida. And I love adventure."

"Nice to meet you," Elsa replied. "This racetrack is a new addition. The track is most fun when visitors like you arrive."

Just then, Dash zipped up to them and came to a stop only long enough to shout, "Race ya! First one to the castle gates wins!"

Everyone smiled. Elsa said, "Let's get going!"

Chapter 2

Dash touched the castle wall first. "Yes!" he shouted.

"You gotta love his enthusiasm," said Mr. Incredible. "He never tires of winning."

"I want a rematch," said Merida to

Dash. "Angus and I nearly won."

"Nearly," said Dash jokingly, looking at Angus, "but not quite!"

Angus whinnied a challenge. The boy and the horse stared each other down, eager for another try.

Elsa came over and introduced herself to Dash. "And since you like moving fast, how about trying out our new ice-skating rink? It's just beyond the castle grounds." As they got to the ice rink,

four Omnidroids raced into the arena. The menacing Omnidroids charged down the rink toward the good guys.

Quick, let's get this spinning." Elsa and Mr. Incredible worked together to spin a giant puck and send it sliding across the ice into an Omnidroid.

"I've got this!" called Elsa. Farther down the ice, near the goal, she double-jumped and attacked one Omnidroid while another swung its metal claws at her. She froze it solid with a blast.

Using his amazing strength, Mr. Incredible smashed the robot's frozen claw, and it shattered to bits. Then another Omnidroid attacked him.

"Take *that*!" called Elsa, sending a frosty white beam toward the Omnidroid attacking Mr. Incredible. The Omnidroid froze in midair—and stayed there!

"Whoa!" said Dash.

They watched as the defeated and frozen Omnidroid fell and rolled to a stop in a heap. "That takes care of that," said Elsa. "For now, anyway.

"Those Omnidroids are always showing up out of nowhere," she went on as they headed back to the castle.

"We know them from home," said Mr. Incredible. "Usually they're the work of Syndrome, our nemesis. We all need to be on the lookout if he's involved."

"Even so," said Dash, "we've got more racing to do. Let's try to forget about bad guys."

"Let's *not* forget," said Merida, "that Angus and I want a rematch."

"You're on!" Dash replied. "The track is waiting."

"Let's *all* race," said Elsa. "It can be a team contest. We'll divide into two teams. Afterward, hot chocolate for everyone!"

Everyone was agreeing that was a wonderful idea, when they heard a *whooooosh* and saw a magic sparkle in the sky near the castle.

"Yes!" Dash cheered. "Those stars always mean something is about to happen! That's how Dad and I got here."

In the glow of the sparkles, two vehicles appeared. One was bright red and shiny, covered in racing stickers. The other was a brown and dusty tow truck.

"Wow!" said Dash. "Impressive!"

"Those vehicles are not behaving . . . *properly,*" said his dad.

"They're not just *vehicles,*" said Elsa. "They have faces, and they're talking to each other!"

"Don't be shy, Mater— Oh, hello!"

The red race car smiled at Elsa.

"Hello there, miss. Good afternoon, and I do very much hope yer having a most *spectaca-lar* day," the tow truck said to Elsa.

"Now that's just overdoing it," Lightning whispered to Mater.

"Welcome to you both," said Elsa, trying not to show that she was quite

surprised to meet two talking vehicles. "I'm Queen Elsa, and this is my home."

"Queen!" said Mater. "This here is Lightning McQueen, and my name's Mater. You all might be related, since you both have 'Queen' in your names."

Elsa laughed. "Pleased to meet you, Mater, and you, too, Lightning. You have arrived at the perfect time. Would you be interested in a race?"

"*Would* we?" Mater replied. "Lightning is the best racer there is."

"*Ka-chow!*" said Lightning. "I'm ready to race right here and right now—wherever *here* is!"

Elsa introduced everyone and

explained that the group was just about to pick teams to have a race. Mater and Lightning were more than happy to join in. They tried to decide on teams, but no one could agree. Elsa came up with a solution.

"Everyone throws or rolls a snowball and tries to hit a certain spot on the ground," she said. "The two who throw the closest to the spot are the captains. To make it fair, I'll throw blindfolded."

The new friends nodded, and Elsa put a stone on the ground as a marker. "Okay, everyone. Get your snowballs ready! Aim for this stone and—*throw*!"

Chapter 3

Dash and Merida got their snowballs closest to the stone and selected their players. Team Dash was Dash, Mr. Incredible, and Mater. Team Merida was Merida, Elsa, and Lightning.

"*Ka-chow!* See you at the finish line,"

said Lightning with a good-natured chuckle.

"See you there!" said Mater. "For some of us, that will be later rather than sooner."

"Wait a minute, please, Lightning," said Elsa. "Let's go to the starting line together."

The starting line of the racetrack was on an elevated spot near the castle. It had a ramp that they could all walk or drive up. At the top of the ramp, they looked down at the racetrack while Elsa described the terrain.

"I have party hats and flags over there by the hot chocolate," Elsa said, pointing to a table. "When you cross the finish line, put on your hat and cheer for your teammates. The first team with all three members to cross the finish line wins!"

For Team Merida, Lightning was revved up and ready at the starting line. Their captain would be riding Angus, while Elsa was set to compete in a vehicle called King Candy's racing kart. For Team Dash, Mr. Incredible was ready to go in his monster truck. Dash didn't use a vehicle because he was a speedy Super. Mater sported some new racing trim to get in the spirit.

From her kart, Elsa raised her hand

and fired a magical blast of snow to start the race. The contestants took off down the track. The road was smooth and wide, and Lightning easily grabbed the lead, followed closely by the Supers, then Elsa, and Merida on Angus. Mater was in the rear.

The track began to rise and turn. The terrain changed and grew woody and icy. The vehicles slipped and slid! Elsa started to spin out of control in her King Candy's kart, but Mr. Incredible nudged it with the front bumper of his monster truck to straighten it out.

"That was mighty nice of you, Mr. Unbelievable, considering Elsa is not on our team," Mater said.

"We're going to win this race fair and square, not because of a traffic accident!" said Mr. Incredible.

Elsa got back on the road, and everyone moved into a new formation: Lightning and Dash at the front, with Dash slightly ahead. The ice delayed Lightning McQueen a bit, but Dash moved so fast that he created heat beneath his feet!

Then came Mr. Incredible and Merida with Angus and, finally, Mater and Elsa.

When they got deep into the woods, a sudden avalanche of rocks showered the track. Lightning saw the danger!

"Watch out, racers!" called the race car from the front.

While the others were distracted by the rocks, Dash and Merida took the lead. Lightning McQueen was determined to catch up—and win!

The track widened on the other side of the bridge and sloped downhill steeply. Lightning could handle the

drop by shifting into a low gear, but the Supers were gaining too much speed!

"Too. Fast. Whoa!" said Dash as he started to lose control.

"Run into a snowbank—that'll stop your momentum!" called his dad.

Meanwhile, beyond the finish line, Lightning and Merida were cheering for Elsa to finish.

Zoom! In came Dash, who crossed the line shouting, "Yesss!" Next came Mr. Incredible.

Elsa stopped to help Mater, who was having engine trouble on the last stretch.

"Dadgum it," said Mater. "You don't

s'pose there's a garage on this track?"

Mater's engine wouldn't start, so Elsa decided to tow him with her kart. She attached his towline to the racer and pulled him across the finish line.

"Team Merida! *Ka-chow!*" shouted Lightning.

Merida whooped. Angus raised his front legs high in the air and whinnied.

"I feel just terrible for losing, Team Dash," said Mater.

Dash walked over to Mater and gave his hood a good-natured punch. "Let's demand a rematch—best of three!"

Mater high-fived Dash with his tow hook.

Chapter 4

"I will say, as the winner," said Lightning McQueen, "that the course was a bit on the easy side. I don't know if you felt that way. . . ."

"Agreed," said Mr. Incredible.

"Aye, we had it won," said Merida.

"All right," said Elsa. "Since, as you all know, this world is filled with toys and vehicles and so many fun things, we could *build* an even more challenging racecourse."

"Make our own racecourse?" asked Dash.

"Yes! With big obstacles and tough challenges—lots of wonderful elements of surprise!"

"What is an *elephant* of surprise?" said Mater.

Just as Mater said the word "surprise," the teams heard a sound that was becoming familiar in this world—a long *whooooosh*—then saw a swirl of sparkling lights.

Out of the lights stepped a young girl with a frying pan. Without taking time to look around, she quickly turned to face six angry-looking guards with helmets—and frying pans—who arrived next to her. The girl fought back as the guards attacked her.

"Wherever they're from, they sure must like to fry things," said Mr. Incredible, cracking his knuckles.

"Let's get 'em!" Merida cried, leading the charge. The two race teams jumped into the fight.

The new girl, who wore a lavender dress, whacked one of her attackers. She called to the friends, "I'm Rapunzel! Thanks for helping me out!"

Elsa froze one of the guards with snowballs. Dash chased another up a hill and forced him into a snowbank.

"Hey, Dash, help me with this catapult," said Mr. Incredible.

"Where'd you find that?" asked

Merida as she fired an arrow at two guards. The arrow ricocheted off the helmet of one and into the other, knocking them both down.

"Ha! You know better than to ask that. In this world, we just find stuff!" Dash picked up a walker with tennis balls on its four metal feet and tripped the last of the guards. "I got him, Dad!"

Rapunzel ran to them. "Thanks, everyone. They've been chasing me since—well, it's a really long story. But trust me, I've gotten used to having bad guys come after me."

The team introduced themselves and asked Rapunzel if she wanted to join the race. The idea excited Rapunzel.

"Which team am I on?" she asked.

"Right now, if we add you, we won't have an even number—"

Suddenly, in a flash of sparkling star light, an alien—or what looked like one—appeared! It was a short, blue-faced creature. And it seemed to have an extra pair of arms.

"I will join," the creature growled.

"Dadgum," said Mater. "Well, take me to your leader."

"Hello, little fella!" said Rapunzel.

"Wow," said Elsa. "Our visitors get more interesting as the day goes on! I'm Elsa. What's your name?"

The creature gurgled and growled.

Rapunzel bent down and shook his hand. "I'm Rapunzel."

The creature said, "Stitch," which they decided was his name. He whipped out a scorecard and looked up at them with pleading eyes.

"Oh, you want to be the judge, do you? Okay, you seem harmless enough," said Elsa.

Then Stitch took a bite out of the scorecard. "Heh-heh," he said.

To make the teams even, Elsa would count twice for Team Merida—as a builder *and* a racer. Team Merida became Merida, Elsa, Lightning, and

Elsa again. Dash's team was Mater, Rapunzel, Mr. Incredible, and Dash.

They decided the strongest team members would build the obstacle courses and the fastest would race. Then each team huddled to choose who would do each job.

"It would be especially fun," said Elsa, "if everyone ran *both* courses. Any challenge one team comes up with, they will also have to face themselves."

"I found these cool scoreboards," said Lightning. Next to him stood a massive scoreboard to keep track of the teams' wins.

"Great! Put that by the finish line," said Elsa.

"We need team flags with our symbols on them!" said Dash. "Ours could be *this*!" He held up a frying pan.

Rapunzel laughed. "Fine with me!"

"Okay, everyone," said Elsa, "we've got all of the castle grounds to build on. That includes the hills and mountains as far as you can see." She pointed to a tall gray mountain standing apart from the other mountains. Its peak was dotted with patches of snow. "Except for that one—we'll have some fun with that later," she told them with a mischievous twinkle in her eye.

Chapter 5

Team Dash and Team Merida took different paths up the snowy hills behind the castle and found the terrain they wanted for their racecourse. They each planted a team flag in the snow. Team Merida had chosen an arrow symbol for their brightly colored flag.

They quickly found ways to unlock catapults, flaming hoops, giant trees, course markers, starting gates, sign-posts, and all the other cool things the wonderful world of the Toy Box offered.

Team Dash's course was built for speed. They were proud of their mega-tall half-pipe. It was three stories high. The racers would have to ride the

half-pipe on hoverboards when they reached that part of the course.

Team Merida's course was all about jumps. A ski jump over a chocolate waterfall was the first big obstacle they dreamed up. And they placed a jump through flaming hoops near the end.

Hours later, when they were done setting everything up, the teams met back at the starting line. Stitch took his place in a beach chair. He was wearing a Hawaiian shirt and sunglasses and playing with a beach ball.

"No fair—he got to sit around while we did all the work," said Dash.

"*Aarrrggghlf!* I will judge," Stitch

replied. "Heh-heh-heh-heh-heh."

Dash frowned at Stitch. The young Super was determined to cross the finish line first.

The teams boarded monster trucks and drove up the mountain to the start of the course. The first racer from each team was ready to go: Merida vs. Mater.

"Merida, you *own* this race," said Lightning, and he flashed her a big smile

"You can do it, Mater!" called Rapunzel. "Stay focused!"

"You betcha, Miss Rapunzel. I am like a laser beam, only not quite that fast . . . or focused." Then he revved his engine, creating a powerful puff of smoke from his tailpipe.

Stitch called from the bottom with a megaphone: "Mark. Set. Fly."

"It's *go,* not fly," called Lightning.

Upon hearing the word "go," Mater began to race. *"Yee-haw!"* he cried as he took off in a cloud of dust.

"Wait!" said Merida. "We haven't started yet."

Mater came to a screeching halt. He almost crashed into a racer who had just come down the hill on a hoverboard. The racer stopped in front of Mater, spraying snow behind her. Then she took off her helmet and shook out her long red hair.

"Hello, friends. I'm Anna, and I live here, too. Do any of you know where I can find my sister, Elsa?"

"Perfect timing," said Elsa, who came over to greet Anna. "The race is just about to start!"

"We divided into teams," Rapunzel said, merrily.

"And built an obstacle course," said Elsa. "Mater and Merida are competing first."

Merida, on a hoverboard, lined up next to Mater.

"Rrrready. Set. Go!" Stitch roared, firing his paintball gun into the air. The racers took off downhill and tried to control their speed.

First up was the chocolate waterfall. They both jumped it easily, but Merida was in the lead. Just as she was about to approach a final jump, a small, unknown racer wearing a mask came whizzing by and crossed in front of her at top speed.

"Watch out!" Merida called. The tiny racer sped away and disappeared. "You almost knocked me over, wee one!"

Merida turned her mind back to the race. She hunched down and tucked herself in tight to gain speed. She pushed her hoverboard to the limit. Heading straight downhill into the final stretch, she sped through to the finish line—the winner!

Chapter 6

Lightning McQueen and Dash raced next. They each ran the course so fast, they were done in a flash. Both had an easy time, not even hitting the markers along the way. Their turns were tight and clean. Lightning enjoyed throwing big waves of snow behind him with his wheels.

But at the finish, Dash crossed just ahead of Lightning.

"Congratulations on a race well run," said Lightning. Then he did a little rev of his engine, and Dash did a victory dance.

"One to one," said Stitch, and he changed the scoreboard.

Elsa lost to Rapunzel, who was an expert climber and could easily handle heights. And instead of jumping through the rings of fire at the end, she had no trouble vaulting over them— which was allowed.

Then Elsa raced again, this time against Mr. Incredible. For all his power, he was not fast on ice. Elsa was an expert at quickly spotting the shiny ice patches and riding over them to pick up speed.

Mr. Incredible had started to gain on her as they approached the downhill finish, when the tiny racer once again barreled toward him from behind a tree. "Whoa!" he cried. He swerved to avoid hitting the mysterious racer.

The near collision with the racer cost Mr. Incredible his momentum, and Elsa took the lead!

"Score: Two. Two," said Stitch as Elsa whizzed across the finish line.

The teams were gathering around the scoreboard when they saw something approaching in the sky. It wasn't a hovercraft or a helicopter— it looked like a superhero!

"It could be one of Syndrome's tricks," said Mr. Incredible.

Mater and Lightning roared their engines, ready to help if the flying object meant trouble.

They all watched as a giant red robot carrying a boy in a purple super suit landed near them. The two newcomers waved.

"We saw your obstacle course from the sky," said the boy. "Looks cool!"

"Perhaps it's time to upgrade our activity matrix to include winter sports," said the big, friendly robot. "Sports improve one's sense of well-being."

"That's another way to say it," said the boy. "That's Baymax—and I'm Hiro. Need some more players?"

"You bet," said Anna. "The game is tied, so we need a tiebreaker."

"*Mount* Tiebreaker, to be exact," said

Elsa. "Made of one hundred percent ice! Come on, everyone, I'll show you!"

"Does this require racing?" Baymax asked. "I am not built for speed."

"I got it, big guy," said Hiro.

The team got on their mounts and followed Elsa. When they reached the top of the hill, they saw a nearby mountain carved out of ice! The ice mountain sparkled with frost—it had ice ramps that twisted and turned. They could see jumps and sheer drops.

"Meet Mount Tiebreaker," said Elsa. "The next level in ice racing. I made it myself."

"Which team am I on, sis?" said Anna.

"You can join Team Merida," said Elsa. "So, Hiro, that means you're on Team Dash."

"Yes!" said Hiro. He fist-bumped Dash. "Victory will be *ours*!"

Chapter 7

As they prepared to face off, Hiro walked over to Anna and said, "May the best racer win."

Baymax powered up his rocket thruster. "It is now safe to board my shoulders."

"He means jump on," Hiro said to Anna. Baymax took them to the top of the glacier, where Elsa was waiting.

Hiro and Anna each stood on their own hoverboard, side by side. They looked down Mount Tiebreaker and saw curving snowbanks, an ice ramp in a 360-degree loop, and big jumps.

"Here we go!" said Hiro. "This super suit hasn't lost yet!"

Elsa gave the word and sent them off with a fresh blast of snow. Down they went, slicing through the course. Their hoverboards swooshed inches above the ice.

Anna and Hiro had just entered the

first jump when both wiped out and landed in a slick patch of ice. Baymax quickly lifted them off the ground. The robot scanned them for injuries, and said, "Your racing competition can now proceed."

"Let's get back to it," said Anna. "I am pretty sure I was just about to leave you in the dust . . . or *frost.*"

Next up was the jump, then the ramps. They whooshed through the half-pipe, Hiro in the lead. But when they got to the multilevel ice ramps, Anna moved out in front.

"Now, this is my kind of race!" she yelled, passing Hiro. The ramps had

steep vertical drops and were super slippery. Hiro went out of control just as the course narrowed into an ice chute. Anna went down the chute first. At the end of it, she saw the finish line. Elsa had created a giant version of Olaf out of building blocks that they had to pass through to get to the finish!

Just then, Hiro zoomed by her. "You snooze, you lose!" he shouted.

"Not snoozing," Anna called after him. "Staring at a giant Olaf!"

Anna watched as Hiro zigzagged across the course below her. His purple super suit was a colorful blur against the white snow. She bent low to increase her speed. "I can't let these tourists win on our ice," she said to herself. "It's a matter of hometown pride!"

Heading into the final section, with the giant Olaf looming below, Anna pulled back into the lead. She could hear Hiro right behind her. The teams were gathered along the final stretch, cheering them on.

"There's an ice waterfall detour, Hiro! Watch out!" shouted Dash.

Lightning called to Anna, "Keep your speed up. And watch the turns!"

The home stretch was a 360-degree ice loop, followed by a vertical plunge. Then the racers would shoot across an ice bridge that sent them through the Olaf statue and to the finish. It was the grand finale of the ice race.

Approaching the 360, Hiro got around Anna. He was used to flying on Baymax's shoulders, so the loop was easy for him.

They were about to shoot down the plunge, when again, the mysterious racer came out of nowhere from a bridge above. The racer knocked into Hiro. He spun out of control.

"Whoa!" Anna cried.

The racer let out a big laugh. "Sweet! No one in any land can outrace me!"

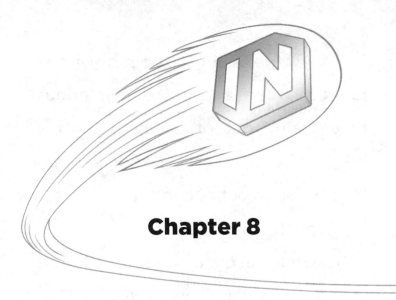

Chapter 8

Just as the new racer was nearing the
finish line, she was joined by another
small and speedy racer—Stitch!

The two of them shot straight over
the ice. Stitch growled with joy. He was
happy to be part of the race.

"Not a judge anymore . . ." he roared. "Stitch will race!" He and the smaller racer crossed paths with Anna and Hiro, beating them by seconds.

Everyone was puzzled. Except Mater.

"Congratulations, tiny lady and blue alien whose name I forgot!" said Mater. "You are one expert racer, little miss. My name's Tow Mater, and that's a fact."

"Vanellope von Schweetz," said the racer. "Winner." She put her hand up for a high five, but no one got her back. "No?"

Hiro and Anna stood behind Vanellope. "Now, wait a second," said Anna. "Just who do you think you are?"

"Hey, I know you!" said the tiny girl, turning around. "We had some *big* fun a while back. Stinky pirates, stinkier super villains, and attacking robots, as I recall."

"Vanellope! Welcome back," Anna said.

"In honor of our surprise winner, I have an idea that includes everyone," said Elsa. "Beyond the big Olaf, inside that sports arena, I've got a special treat."

They made their way over to the arena and went inside. The huge stadium was filled with cheering spectators. There was an ice rink, plus hockey pucks and all kinds of toys and sports equipment—and hot chocolate for everyone.

"I figured an ice party was in order," said Elsa.

Everyone reached for a steaming cup of hot chocolate. The delicious drink was just what everyone needed after the day's challenges.

"But we don't have a clear winner," said Mr. Incredible. "This is not protocol."

"Not at all," said Lightning, "but I'm getting the hang of racing just for fun. We're all winners here—right, buddy?"

"You betcha," said Mater. "Now I'm going to try some of that hot brown gasoline in a cup!"

"Well, technically, Stitch and I *are* the winners," Vanellope said.

"We're all winners, so let's have some fun," said Elsa before anyone could complain. She jumped onto a giant hockey puck. Mr. Incredible

pushed it toward the goal. When she crossed the goal line, the audience cheered and the scoreboard lit up.

Soon all the racers were playing.

"I was kind of mad at first," Hiro told Vanellope. "But this is even better than racing." He and Baymax were pushing her on one of the giant hockey pucks.

"Trust me," she said. "*Everything* is fun in this world."

"Excuse me," said Dash, nudging Hiro out of the way. He spun the giant hockey puck at super speed, and Vanellope laughed as she held on tight.

After the giant ice party, the group was tired but happy from their long day of racing and play. Stars began to appear, and everyone felt a pull toward home.

"I'll miss this place," said Rapunzel. "But I think it's time for me to leave."

"Me too," said Merida. "Angus and I need to go home. We've been gone a wee bit too long."

"Well, we're sure going to miss all of you," said Lightning. "But we see our star, so it's back to Radiator Springs for Mater and me."

"Goodbye, everyone," said Dash. "I still want a rematch!"

"I think we'll see these good citizens again," said Mr. Incredible, putting his hand on Dash's shoulder. "Goodbye for now!"

Vanellope turned and said goodbye, too. "Thanks for being good sports about the race," she said to the sisters. Then she added, *"I'll be back."*

Anna and Elsa watched as the stars twinkled, and they knew their adventure had come to an end. "Race you home?" Elsa said.

Anna laughed. "I thought I was done with racing for today—but why not? First sister to the castle wins!" she said. And off they sped.

When they reached the castle door, they sank to the ground, out of breath,

and laughed about all the adventures they'd had.

"Mater was so sweet!" said Elsa.

"And what about the ride on the huge robot?" said Anna.

Just then, Baymax and Hiro flew over the castle and landed in front of them.

"Yes, we're like the guests who don't know when to leave," Hiro said. "But it seems like there might be another adventure just waiting to happen."

"Of course! It would be fun to have you join us," said Elsa. "We can pretend to be superheroes like you!"

"You're on," said Hiro, smiling.

"I will load a training module to

prepare for the next adventure," said Baymax. "Fist bumps for everyone are now recommended."

THE END?